W9-COZ-582

Pinocchio

A Tale of Honesty

Retold by Tom DeFalco
Illustrated by Tom Leigh

Famous Fables

Reader's Digest Young Families

Once there was an old man named Geppetto who carved toys and puppets out of wood. He loved children and had always wanted a son. One day he made a special puppet for himself and named him "Pinocchio."

That night the Blue Fairy visited Geppetto while he was asleep. She wanted to reward him for being such a good person. She waved her magic wand and Pinocchio sprang to life. Although he was made of wood, Pinocchio could see, hear, talk, and move like a real boy.

Geppetto was very happy when he saw that Pinocchio had come to life. "You should go to school," said the old man. "You will make friends and learn many wonderful things. Be careful, Pinocchio," said Geppetto. "Do not talk to any strangers on the way to school."

But Pinocchio did not pay attention to what his father said. On the road he stopped to talk with a sly fox and a crafty cat.

"Forget about school!" said the fox. "You'll have to sit in a chair and do work. Even worse, you'll have to be quiet! We're going to a puppet show. Come with us and you'll have fun."

Pinocchio wanted to have fun, so he went with the fox and the cat.

When the owner of the puppet show saw Pinocchio, he was astonished and quick to realize his good fortune. "A puppet without strings!" he exclaimed. "People will come from miles around to see such an amazing sight! He will be the star of my show and make me rich." The man picked up Pinocchio and locked him in a cage. "You belong to me now, and I will never let you go."

Pinocchio thought he would never see Geppetto again. He cried and cried. After a while, the Blue Fairy appeared. "Why are you in this cage?" she asked.

Pinocchio feared the Blue Fairy would be angry with him if he told her the truth. So he made up a story. As he told his tale, his wooden nose grew longer and longer. "What is wrong with my nose?" he asked.

"One lie leads to another," explained the Blue Fairy. "A lie keeps growing like the nose on your face."

"I did not know lying was wrong. I won't tell a lie again," Pinocchio promised.

The Blue Fairy waved her magic wand. Pinocchio was set free and his nose returned to its normal size.

As Pinocchio ran toward Geppetto's shop, he met the fox and the cat again.

"Why are you in such a hurry to get home? Your father will only send you back to school," they said. "Come with us to the Island of Fun."

Pinocchio forgot all about going to school and took the boat to the Island of Fun. Once on the island, the boys had a grand time. They played all day and long into the night.

At dinnertime, the boys were thrilled to find that only desserts were served! They stuffed themselves until they fell asleep.

When Pinocchio woke up, he discovered that something terrible had happened. Because he had been so naughty, he had grown long ears and a tail!

As Pinocchio stood on the beach confused and unhappy, he saw Geppetto approaching in a small boat. But then a huge whale arose and swallowed the boat in one giant gulp!

Without a thought for his own safety, Pinocchio dove into the water to save his father. At that very moment, the Blue Fairy appeared and rewarded Pinocchio's unselfishness. She waved her magic wand and Pinocchio's donkey ears and tail vanished. The Blue Fairy watched until Pinocchio safely reached the giant whale and swam into its mouth.

Deep in the belly of the whale, Pinocchio found Geppetto unharmed. "I'm sorry for behaving so badly," Pinocchio said. "I promise to be a good boy. Now we must find a way out of here."

Pinocchio and Geppetto waited until the huge whale yawned. Then they swam out into the ocean as fast as they could.

When Pinocchio and Geppetto returned home, the Blue Fairy appeared again. "Your deeds show how much you love one another. And thus, I have a special reward for you both," she said.

With a wave of her magic wand, the Blue Fairy transformed Pinocchio from a wooden puppet into a real boy. From then on, Pinocchio always went to school and never told a lie. He and Geppetto lived happily ever after.

Famous Fables, Lasting Virtues

Tips for Parents

Now that you've read Pinocchio, *use these pages as a guide in teaching your child the virtues in the story. By talking about the story and its message and engaging in the suggested activities, you can help your child develop good judgment and a strong moral character.*

About Honesty

It can be distressing for parents to learn that their child has not told the truth. However, there are some common reasons why children are dishonest:

1. They are trying to stay out of trouble or avoid getting punished.
2. They're worried about disappointing you.
3. They're trying to avoid being embarrassed.
4. They're looking for attention.
5. They don't understand the difference between reality and fantasy.

It's important to remember that most children under the age of six or seven do not yet fully understand the difference between reality and fantasy. Sometimes adults encourage the two to blend, as when we talk about Santa Claus, the Tooth Fairy, the Easter Bunny and other imaginary characters. So if your young child has not yet sorted out the difference, it is not a reason for concern or for punishment.

Try to avoid asking a question that might lead your child to tell a lie. ("Did you hit your sister?") Rather, show you are interested in learning the truth about what occurred, and that it's important for everyone in the family to be responsible for what they have done. ("I see you two are having some trouble getting along. I'd like each of you to tell me what happened.")

The best way to raise honest children is to give them positive messages about themselves, praise them as often as possible, and be honest yourself.